PLAY THE RIGHT CARD

A DELTA FORCE ROMANCE STORY

M. L. BUCHMAN

Buchman Bookworks

Other works by M. L. Buchman:

<u>The Night Stalkers</u>

MAIN FLIGHT
The Night Is Mine
I Own the Dawn
Wait Until Dark
Take Over at Midnight
Light Up the Night
Bring On the Dusk
By Break of Day

WHITE HOUSE HOLIDAY
Daniel's Christmas
Frank's Independence Day
Peter's Christmas
Zachary's Christmas
Roy's Independence Day
Damien's Christmas

AND THE NAVY
Christmas at Steel Beach
Christmas at Peleliu Cove

5E
Target of the Heart
Target Lock on Love
Target of Mine

<u>Firehawks</u>

MAIN FLIGHT
Pure Heat
Full Blaze
Hot Point
Flash of Fire
Wild Fire

SMOKEJUMPERS
Wildfire at Dawn
Wildfire at Larch Creek
Wildfire on the Skagit

<u>Delta Force</u>
Target Engaged
Heart Strike
Wild Justice

<u>White House Protection Force</u>
Off the Leash
On Your Mark
In the Weeds

<u>Where Dreams</u>
Where Dreams are Born
Where Dreams Reside
Where Dreams Are of Christmas
Where Dreams Unfold
Where Dreams Are Written

<u>Eagle Cove</u>
Return to Eagle Cove
Recipe for Eagle Cove
Longing for Eagle Cove
Keepsake for Eagle Cove

<u>Henderson's Ranch</u>
Nathan's Big Sky
Big Sky, Loyal Heart

<u>Love Abroad</u>
Heart of the Cotswolds: England
Path of Love: Cinque Terre, Italy

<u>Dead Chef Thrillers</u>
Swap Out!
One Chef!
Two Chef!

<u>Deities Anonymous</u>
Cookbook from Hell: Reheated
Saviors 101

<u>SF/F Titles</u>
The Nara Reaction
Monk's Maze
the Me and Elsie Chronicles

<u>Strategies for Success (NF)</u>
Managing Your Inner Artist/Writer
Estate Planning for Authors

The flash of white-gold drew Ramiro's attention from the *mote de queso*.

It was a soup he'd lifted from Colombia's Caribbean Coast and was adapting to the Medellín palate—with his own modern style of course. The thick hard cheese had been transformed to tiny floating islands that would catch in every spoonful. The sweetness of yam now came from roasted and juiced corn, and the coconut milk base was reconstructed from goat milk and white chocolate.

It was close. So close. It needed more roasted-corn milk—and, he tried not to sigh, less salt. Nowhere in Colombia was there a love for the salt and sweet together as there was in Medellín, but the balance was wrong. The only way to put less in was to start over and he'd already been nursing this soup along for two days. Any distraction was welcome.

The flash of white-gold was a man's pale blond hair. Not exactly common in the heart of the Santo Domingo district of Medellín. It belonged to a big guy. Tall and incredibly broad of shoulder. The man who followed him in was darker, but no smaller. They looked like two tanks rolling into his restaurant. Ramiro didn't need to be brilliant to spot American drug-war military.

"*Buenos días, amigos.* Welcome to my restaurant." He worked hard on his English hoping for just this moment. American military liked to think they were adventurous, but they rarely were. It had taken three months for one to walk in here. If he could make a good impression, they'd tell their friends and then he'd be made. The *barrio*'s locals were fine, but money came from the Americans. Also if the Americans came, then the trendy Paisas from lower Medellín would start riding the tram or the escalator up into the *barrio* and they too had money.

"Hey there." The blond man offered one of those odd, meaningless American greetings as they looked around.

The *barrio* of Santo Domingo had changed so much since the days when Pablo Escobar's drug money had ruled here, that the neighborhood of his youth was almost unrecognizable. There were still alleys and streets that even he didn't walk into, but no longer did everyone spend whole days cowering out of sight as gun battles raged along the *Fronteras Invisibles* that had divided the drug militias' territories. With new parks, libraries, civic centers, and even massive outdoor escalators that climbed right up into the hills of the upper *comunas,* the neighborhoods had slowly quieted and were regaining cohesion, like a fine sauce.

It wasn't done yet, but gunfire was now less common than bombs had been the year when six thousand had died in this city alone. The lower city was far safer and the hill neighborhoods were following.

Ramiro had done his best to make his restaurant fit the modern times. The walls were white, with paintings of local vistas—cheap ones from street artists but with a sharp, modernist eye. The tables were topped with black Formica and dark blue linoleum covered the old wood floors. The chairs he'd selected for comfort over style. This restaurant was his very breath, and his future.

"Would you like some lunch, my friends?" Please let them be his friends. He moved out to escort them to seats. There were ten tables and only two were occupied, so where they sat didn't matter; the secret was to get them sitting.

"Sure. Duane says he's ready to eat a horse. Me, I'm fine with just a small cow or two." Their Spanish was very good, though strangely regionless. It didn't matter, it made his life easier. He still had to concentrate to get English syntax organized in his head before he spoke.

When he tried to hand over menus, the blond guy waved them away. "You're the chef, you choose. We're not picky eaters."

"*I'm* not," 'Duane' grumbled out in a voice that sounded little used. "Chad's got this thing against *aji chombo* sauce."

"Only because the last time you said 'Try it, you'll like it,' it burned a hole in my tongue that came out through the bottom of my boots. I liked those boots."

"He likes wearing ballet slippers."

Ramiro knew it was bad form to laugh in a customer's face—especially one he wanted to turn into a repeat customer—but he couldn't help himself.

"That's ballet *dancers*. Those girls bring a whole new meaning to flexible. And I won't mention Duane and his bunny slippers," blond 'Chad's' smile forgave Ramiro his laugh.

Ramiro wasn't sure what "bunny slippers" were. He wondered if they used their real names. Probably. Duane's tan was dark enough, but Chad would never pass as undercover anything in Colombia. Time to get back to the food.

"The reason you don't like the *aji chombo* is because you eat the Venezuelan sauce." Venezuela was just another confirmation of who they were as it was a border that was not very comfortable to cross right now. "You must try my *aji picante Colombiano.* It is hot, but it is not simply hot with peppers. It is hot with *flavor.* It is hot with the spirit of Colombia."

"Bring it on, brother." Duane turned to his friend, "You got the cards?"

"You were supposed to— Shit, bro." He turned to Ramiro. "Do you have any playing cards?"

Ramiro went to look, but all he found were a pack of My Little Pony cards his niece had left behind on her last visit from Bogota.

"Sorry, all I could find, my friends."

Chad fanned the deck. Ramiro should have told them he couldn't find anything. They'd take offense at these silly pink cards and walk away.

Brightly colored cartoon ponies adorned them. The suits were made up of hearts, diamonds, rainbows, and more. A "three of butterflies" flew around the image of Fluttershy, a beige pony with hot pink hair. A "seven of balloons" floated above the wild-eyed party pony Pinkie Pie with her hot pink hair. He and Marie had played the game for endless hours. Those days had gone by far too fast. No little girl of his own to raise. No little boy to follow in his footsteps. Not yet anyway, but Marie made him wish.

But these military men were not eight-year old Marie.

It was a disaster before he'd even served the first plate. They'd never come back. He—

Chad quickly chucked aside the eights, nines, and tens, then began shuffling the deck. Truco? Two American military men were going to play a vicious, cut-throat game like Truco with My Little Pony cards.

They seemed to forget about his existence, so he slowly eased away and almost landed in Jesús Rivera's lap, which would have been very bad. He'd known Jesús since they were kids, but his was the last major drug militia still working Santo Domingo. He'd become so hard over the years that Ramiro had barely recognized him when he returned from his apprenticeship and cooking school in Bogotá.

Ramiro hurried back to the kitchen.

*E*stela had watched the Americans stroll past the front of her restaurant without thinking anything of it. But when news had spread—as quickly as everything in the *barrio* did—of a noisy two-person game of Truco in Ramiro's *Restaurante de Medellín*, she had her suspicions. When Marla came in for an order of *chicharrón* with a side of beans and rice to take to her ailing father—who had made a profession of ailing ever since his daughter had married well enough to support him—and asked how it was possible for hair to be so close to white on a young and handsome man, it only confirmed what Estela already knew.

The Americans wanted to eat at Ramiro's? It was their loss. It wasn't authentic Colombian food. It was barely food according to some of her customers. She didn't need more customers. Even Ramiro returning from the big city with his big city ideas and moving in next door hadn't worried her.

The *Paisas* of Medellín—the real locals—knew real food. She and Cara could barely keep up with the crowded tables. Those who had to wait were always offered a *jugó* of iced juice mixed with coconut milk. She knew the feeding and keeping of customers far better than Ramiro with his fancy molecules and *espuma* that he dropped in frothy little piles as if a person could be satisfied with air and bubbles.

He knew nothing.

Then why did the Americans eating there irk her so?

She paused in the kitchen long enough to drink a lime and coconut *jugó* herself as the thin-sliced plantain *patacones* fried for the second time. Her *restaurante* was warm compared to Ramiro's chilly *moderno* nonsense. The wood walls had been placed here by her grandfather. Her grandmother had fed the people of Santo Domingo at these same wooden tables. Even when Pablo Escobar and the other murderous drug scum had ruled the streets, people still had to eat.

She had learned that lesson to her very soul on the day that a bomb killed her mother as she walked along the street with a basket of chicken and potatoes. The explosion had also killed the children of a police captain. It was the day that Estela's schooling *and* childhood had ended. She and Nana had run the restaurant from the very next day, *because the people they must eat, si?* Now this place was hers. No, it was *her*. She and her restaurant were one and the same. It was something else she had learned from Nana.

She didn't need Ramiro. She didn't care about his food that wasn't food. And she certainly didn't miss the few people who went to his restaurant when hers was crowded for hours every mealtime.

"What's on the menu today, Estela?" She knew the voice without turning.

"Nothing for you, Jesús Rivera. Ever. I told you not to come in here." She rattled the basket in the frying oil.

"Why don't you like me, Estela? I can show you a very good time. Take you away from all this sweaty work. All these people." *All these people* was precisely why she was here.

She loved serving traditional, hearty food to the *Paisas* of Medellín.

She had told him a thousand times no. They had all grown up together here: her, Ramiro, Jesús, and so many others. Many were dead in the drug wars, some had left, very few had come back like Ramiro. She had thought him long gone and wished him well away. It was only after he left that she'd come to miss him. He had been a young man of dreams.

Jesús had just become a runner for the local drug militia back then—still called Pablo's Domingo Guerrilleros even after Escobar's death. Jesús' *compañeros*, though, had boasted loudly of killing the police captain's children. All of her begging had brought no police to the *barrio* seeking justice. She had even gone to Jesús as a friend. At the age of fourteen, he had tried to set the price for helping her as having his way with her. When she had refused, he had slapped her face so hard that it had hurt for a week. She'd given him his first knife scar in payback. Jesús was now the Guerrilleros' leader.

He would be leaning on the small service counter that separated her kitchen from the crowd. Everyone would be watching, of course. The rapidly quieting restaurant all remembered how she and Jesús had run together as children. She wondered how much money had changed hands over the years betting on if, or when, Jesús would bed her.

Not now. Not ever.

She dipped the empty wire basket deep in the frying oil and tipped her head for several seconds as if considering how to respond to him. The restaurant was stone silent now in anticipation of her answer, but that couldn't be helped.

Yanking the basket from the oil, she tapped it once to clear the drips before whirling on him to hold it less than an inch from his smug face. His smugness disappeared fast enough.

"The answer, Jesús, is that there is *nothing* on the menu

here for you. Not me, not a bowl of *mondongo* soup, not a glass of juice. If you come in my restaurant again, you will wear a seared print of this basket on your face until the end of your days."

He held her gaze and she wondered how crazy a risk she'd just taken.

They held each other's glare until a single drip of hot oil fell from the basket onto the back of his hand where it rested on the counter.

His yelp of surprise and jerk backwards elicited a laugh from the gathered diners. Jesús gave her a look darker than the ancient iron of her grill and stalked out the door. A hubbub of speculations among the diners washed across the tables. Some thought it was the next step in an on-going courtship. Others felt that it was proof that it was all decided for now and ever. Only one or two eyed her with caution.

Yes, if they were smart, they would stay away for a while. There was no doubt in her mind, the worst was yet to come.

As she returned to her cooking, she considered her options, but they were few and far between. She was alone now. Oh, she had many friends in the community, but most of those were smart enough to still fear Jesús Rivera and the remains of the Domingo Guerrilleros. Her grandmother had died of old age, her father during an accident in the oil fields, and her mother by that bomb.

Who could help her?

The scene with her and Jesús complete, at least for now, conversation slowly shifted back to speculating about the two men eating at Ramiro's. They fit none of the standard tourist stereotypes except for being American and where they chose to eat. That implied they were US military.

There was no question, at least not in the hilltop *barrios* of Medellín, that it had been America's Delta Force who finally took down Escobar. The trademark sharpshooting was proof enough, even without what those on the street had seen. The Colombian police had tried—at least the ones not too afraid of retribution had tried—but the shot to the head as Pablo had raced across uneven roof tiles was too neat, too perfect. And the small American team who had been haunting Medellín for months had disappeared that night.

The two Americans. They weren't merely US military. Delta Force was back in Santo Domingo. If there was anyone to stop Jesús, they were the men to do it.

How to get their attention?

She was pretty enough to get any man's attention—Jesús had only been one of the many who followed her about in their youth and since. But there was a *far* more reliable way to get any man's attention, especially the kind of attention she wanted.

3

"Hey, Ramiro. You still got that girlie deck of cards?"

Ramiro looked up in delight. He hadn't expected the Americans to come back the very next day. And for dinner, which was even better than lunch. His ploy had worked. He had cooked for them like he'd never cooked before—though he wished he hadn't given in to the temptation to serve his salty soup. It was the only dish they had neither remarked on nor finished.

"Dickhead forgot them again," Chad hooked a thumb over his shoulder, but no one was there. Duane must be outside, maybe with more of their friends.

"Sure, here you go, *mi amigo.*" He tossed the pack over the counter.

"Thanks. I'll get them back to you."

Ramiro could only gawk in surprise as Chad strode back out the door. Ramiro hurried past the few diners lingering over dessert and looked out just in time to see Chad turn into Estela's restaurant.

"*No! Imposible!*" He couldn't breathe against the pressure

in his chest. How had that woman bewitched *his* Americans? The same way she'd bewitched him and every other person in all Santo Domingo since she'd learned to walk. He'd become a cook to impress her. And when that hadn't worked, he'd left and studied to become a chef. He had taken over the building next door to hers so that he could show her just who could cook now. Not that she seemed to be succumbing to his grand plan.

But to steal his Americans was beyond unfair.

Cara, her waitress, stepped out the front door to set some folding chairs and a card table on the sidewalk in front of Estela's restaurant. With the hot sun setting, it would be as cool and inviting here as the inside of her restaurant had always been. The Garcia family stepped out of the restaurant and sat at the table—all seven of them crowded together. That would be a nice ticket, even at Estela's low prices. He glanced in through the small window. The place teemed with people. His Americans were in a corner near the kitchen, completely out of reach, wielding his niece's My Little Pony cards as if they were weapons of war. Their game of Truco now had numerous spectators.

Estela came out balancing great platters of empanadas and salsas for the Garcias. Only as she finished serving them did she turn and see him.

"Ramiro," she offered him one of those amazing, friendly smiles that made him forgive her everything.

Except this time.

He steeled his inner resolve, but could only manage one word.

"How?" he waved a hand toward the window.

Her lovely brow furrowed for only a moment. "Oh. The Delta Force men."

"They're not—" But Estela had always been the smartest

chica in school, until the day she had to leave to work here. If she said that's what they were, they must be. "*Sí.* Them."

"I offered them each one of my *obleas* for dessert when they left your restaurant yesterday, then invited them to come back the next time they were hungry."

"That's not fair, Estela." Nobody made an *oblea* as good as Estela. Each wafer was bigger around than the tips of his spread fingers and thinner than a whisper. She built them in layers of jam, then wafer, then salty white cheese, another wafer, thickened cream, and so on until they were an inch thick. Sweet, salty, thick, crunchy—it was every possible flavor and texture in each delicate bite.

She gave him an unreadable look.

"You know what this means, don't you?" And he stalked back to his own restaurant. If it was war she wanted, he'd bring it and bring it hard.

$\mathcal{E}$stela watched Ramiro go and tried not to feel the ache in her heart. He had been so strange since his return that in some ways she no longer knew him. Where was the boy whose eyes had followed her even when he himself hadn't dared? It had taken her until he had left to understand that perhaps the quiet boy was the good one and the ones who were so brash and confident—especially those waving about their drug wealth—were *not* so kind. But now?

Now Ramiro would barely speak with her. And somehow, her seeking the protection of the Americans was yet another offense. She would have to do something about that —when she didn't have a restaurant crowded with customers and Jesús to worry about.

The dinner service ran by so fast as it always did when she was busy. She was outside in the soft twilight, cleaning up the dishes when a hand grabbed her wrist forcing her to drop a plate that shattered on the rough street. She knew it immediately by the long, thin cruelty of the fingers that her cheek still remembered from all those years ago.

"It's time, *chica,*" Jesús breathed in her ear as his other hand clamped about her waist from behind. "It is time you finally gave me what is mine."

She was helpless against his whipcord strength.

His hand shifted over her mouth. She tried to bite it, but he was expecting that and merely wrenched her neck harder as he forced her to walk ahead of him down the street.

He was going to rape her in some back alley. And she was going to fight until he was forced to kill her to do so. For all her struggles, she might as well have been a fly to be shooed away from a hock of raw lamb.

Tears began to stream down her face. To end like this was too horrible for thought. If she could die right here, right now, shredded by a bomb like her mother, she would take that over what awaited her at Jesús' hands.

Then, by some miracle, it happened. She was slammed down onto the street. But she wasn't dead. Her ears didn't bleed from the blast of the bomb.

At the sound of the snarl behind her, she rolled over and saw Jesús' back. And beyond him she saw the two Delta men.

"Looky here, buddy," the blond one had his hands tucked into his back pockets. "We've got someone who isn't playing nice. He's trying to take away the chef before we get another one of her *obleas*."

"Doesn't seem right," the darker one agreed. There was a gun in his hand, but he was holding it oddly. More as if he'd snatched it out of Jesús' waistband than if he'd pulled his own from some hidden spot. With three gestures so fast that she couldn't follow them, he separated the gun into four pieces. He pocketed one piece, threw a pair of them into a garbage can, and chucked the last into one of the neighborhood's brand new storm drains where it rattled away.

Jesús yanked out a knife and flicked it open. She wanted to warn them, he was an expert knife fighter, just as his father had been when he was one of Escobar's actual bodyguards. But the cry caught in her throat. She had scarred Jesús' face with that knife when she was twelve. And now he was going to carve up these men whose help she needed but hadn't had time to ask.

And then he was going to carve her.

"Aw, ain't he cute," the blond one had no idea the danger he was in. "He's got a pig sticker."

"More like a guinea pig sticker," the darker one answered.

"Maybe it's a mouse sticker."

Neither man had the sense to reach for a gun. If they really were Delta Force, they must have guns.

The next moment happened so fast, she could never quite make sense of it.

"Pitiful, dude," the blond one sounded bored and walked by Jesús as if he wasn't even there. He bent down to offer her his hand with his back to the most dangerous knife fighter in the *barrio*, perhaps in Medellín.

Jesús moved to take advantage.

Before she could scream a warning, the darker one stepped forward. One moment Jesús was lunging with his knife. The next he was pinned with his back against the wall, his feet off the ground, and the only sound in the night was his knife clattering down upon a stone. His knife hand was clutched tightly in his other hand as if it was in great pain.

"Little boys shouldn't play with knives," the blond one winked at her as he helped her to her feet, only then turning to see what had happened.

With no apparent effort, the darker one lifted Jesús clear of the wall, then tossed him into the same garbage can where parts of his gun had been thrown.

The blond one picked up the blade and inspected it carefully.

"A gift from Escobar to his father," she told him.

"A custom Terzuola. One of his early designs. Make for a good souvenir."

"He was generous with his men." There were still people who worshipped Escobar. He had brought the first lights to a Medellín soccer field so that the locals could play at night. He gave gifts to his adherents so that they lived like kings. And threw lavish parties for "his people"—the *Paisas* of the *barrio*.

"And lethal to his enemies." The blond folded the blade back into the handle with a practiced flick then offered it to her.

She shook her head. "I want no part of the past. Medellín is better with his death. The narco-tourists—they should all live as I did. All die as my mother did. Then we would see if they think it is so fascinating."

He nodded, instead tossing her the deck of brightly cheerful cards they'd been using to play Truco. "Could you make sure these get back to Ramiro?" They walked her back to her restaurant, waved, and disappeared into the night.

Estela was done with the past. In so many ways.

She looked in, saw that Cara was almost done cleaning the restaurant. When she waved through the window, she received a cheery wave back. No one was the wiser for tonight's events, which was a blessing.

The bright lights still streamed out onto the rough pavement from *Restaurante de Medellín*. She stepped into that bright light, then into Ramiro's restaurant. She had never actually been in here. She didn't understand the stark colors and sharp edges, but she'd seen his prices and his clientele dressed in their expensive clothes.

"Is this the future?" She wondered aloud.

Ramiro twisted around from where he was resetting a last table, making sure the linen tablecloth—an actual tablecloth—was arranged just so.

5

———————

"One version of it." Ramiro could feel the bitterness in his voice, but it was hard to feel it when he looked at her. She wore the simplest of clothes, a voluminous red skirt in her grandmother's village's pattern that she made beautiful rather than mundane. Her white blouse, its collar and sleeves embroidered with tiny red roses, hung loosely over her generous figure until it gathered in the skirt at her trim waist. Her long dark hair framed a face so lovely that Prieto might have painted it, if Estela hadn't so brought so much life to it herself.

Her eyes seemed a little wider than usual, as if she'd just been running and was surprised to find herself breathless.

"Feed me your food, Ramiro. Show me what it is you do."

In a dream, he pulled aside a seat for her and held it out.

She shook her head, her hair now loose rather than in the generous ponytail he'd seen earlier, she moved up to the counter facing the kitchen to sit at one of the stools. She made a show of placing two napkins—one in front of her and one at the stool beside her, then set down the deck of My Little Pony playing cards.

"They're gone?"

She nodded.

He searched for anger, but couldn't seem to find it.

He started with the soup he had rebuilt from scratch. It was still young—two more days simmering and the broth would truly meld—but the salt and the sweet, the fruit and the cheese were finally in the right balance.

She tasted. With her soft sigh as encouragement, he moved on to rock shrimp steamed in hearts of palm with a pineapple foam. Shaved New York strip served on yucca bread with liquid nitrogen crystalized guacamole shards and seared discs of *chicharón*. She said nothing, but she finished everything down to the last fork-clattering scrape of the plate. The meal stretched long into the night as he made only one course and two plates at a time, then sat to share it with her. Only when they were done, did he rise to start the next course.

Finally he made dessert—his version of an *oblea*.

The wafer was seasoned with fine-grated candied ginger and the tiniest shreds of dark-roasted habanero and red bell pepper so that it almost sparkled with color. He had deconstructed the elements of salt and sweet, savory and umami, *crema de leche* and merest slivers of aged ham. He had stayed up through the night using all of his skills to create it, to win the Americans back from Estela. Never in a thousand years had he imagined that he would be making it for her instead. He served it on a clean white plate in neatly sliced pie sections rather than the traditional full round wrapped in foil.

When he served it on the single plate and set it between their places, it felt as if all the life had gone out of him. He couldn't even find the energy to lift a slice for himself. Instead, he sat and watched as Estela bit off the end of one of the slices with her perfect white teeth. She closed her eyes as she chewed and, he hoped, savored.

She set it down after only the one lone bite.

"You don't like it." She had always been the best cook he'd ever known. They had sung his praises in Bogotá, but none of that mattered. What mattered was what Estela thought. And she had set it down after one bite.

Then she slipped a finger under his chin and forced him to look up at her. It might be the first time they had ever touched.

"How?"

How had he failed? He didn't know. "I was trying—" *foolishly* "—to impress you. That was always why I cooked. You remember how my father would beat me, but I never let you know why. It was because I wouldn't join a cartel and take the easy drug money, instead I cooked. For you."

Her thumb brushed his cheek so gently.

If he was any less of a man, he would cry. But he had his pride, and that didn't include crying in front of Estela. He would leave. He would take the remains of his meager savings and go back to Bogotá. There he would open a restaurant in the finest neighborhood where they understood him, rather than some *barrio* where he no longer belonged.

Her kiss was flavored with his *oblea*.

Estela's lips were softer and warmer than he'd ever imagined. They were like her cooking, so complete and perfect that he didn't know why he'd ever even tried to compete.

She eased back ever so slightly, but still her hand was on his cheek.

"It was amazing, Ramiro. You captured the flavors of the *Paisa*—the flavor of the people—but somehow you brought it a new life without losing the heart of the food. And I will never make another *oblea* when I could have one of yours instead."

"It was all for you, Estela. You're the only thing I ever wanted."

She smiled. "I understand that now." And she leaned back in for another kiss.

He closed his eyes just as their lips met and—

A hand grabbed him by the scruff of the neck and tossed him aside. He crashed into the line of stools and landed in a painful tangle on the floor.

"Don't be taking what's mine, Ramiro. You know better than that."

Jesús Rivera tipped up a stool and dropped into it beside Estela. He reached out with a hand and grabbed a fistful of Estela's hair, but hissed with pain as if she had spikes in it.

"Hand hurting, Jesús?" Estela's sarcasm earned her a sharp slap across the jaw with the back of his other hand.

"No *Americano* here to protect you now."

And Ramiro understood.

Estela hadn't been trying to steal his Americans. She had recognized Delta Force operators and gambled that they were the only ones skilled enough to take on Jesús. He had not become the leader of Pablo's Domingo Guerrilleros with his gentle ways—he'd left a trail of the scarred, the crippled, and the dead in the wake of his success.

But they weren't here now.

Ramiro tried to move silently, but was too tangled in the stools.

"Get me something to drink." Jesús didn't even bother to turn. Neither did he release his fistful of Estela's hair.

Ramiro could feel Estela's eyes on him as he stepped through the gap in the counter and found a bottle of Aguardiente. Ramiro of the past would have served it in a glass.

Would have scurried away and tried not to think about what Jesús did to his women.

But that was a Ramiro he no longer knew. Estela had kissed him. Had told him without words that she loved his food. And that maybe, just maybe she had real feelings for him.

He uncorked the bottle and set it on the counter by Jesús. He could see Estela's eyes die a little as Ramiro backed away. As Jesús would expect.

Backed away, while Jesús twisted Estela's head cruelly one way and another. Backed away until his hand landed exactly where he intended, on the ten-inch chef's knife that he always put in the same precise spot on his counter.

By shifting behind Jesús, he blocked Estela's view of him. Then, lunging through the server's gap in the counter, he plunged the knife into Jesús' back. It was like plunging it into stone. The shock slammed up his arm as Jesús roared in fury. He spun on Ramiro as the small stream of blood ran down from his shoulder blade.

Stupid. He should have thought about a man's anatomy. Where were you supposed to stab a man? How would he know? In the kidneys might have been good if he had thought of it in time. Instead his knife had bounced off Jesús' shoulder blade and only infuriated him.

His punch slammed Ramiro back against his stove; the pain such an explosion that he could only collapse to the floor.

Jesús was also screaming in pain, holding his hand close to his chest. But his face was almost black with rage. Jesús bent down to pick up the knife that the force of Ramiro's attack had knocked out of his hand. There was no question he was about to die on his own blade.

Unwilling to witness his own death, he squeezed his eyes shut against the coming blow.

Then he heard a deep voice. "Thought we told you that little boys shouldn't play with knives."

Jesús' roared with fury. Ramiro opened his eyes and managed to lean far enough to look through the counter's gap. The Americans caught Jesús' charge as if he was a butterfly on one of the My Little Pony cards.

"Didn't realize you were Jesús Rivera," Chad continued. "Been looking for you for a bit. Might have saved these folks some trouble if you'd bothered to introduce yourself earlier. Excuse us." He offered both Estela and him pleasant nods as if they were passing each other on the street.

They marched Jesús out the door and into the night.

Rumors sprang up of magnificent final gun battles or dark American prisons, but no one ever saw Jesús Rivera again.

Ramiro and Estela had kept their thoughts to themselves.

Months later, Ramiro could only wonder at Estela's brilliance. She had been right as usual. He had wanted to cut a wide arch between their restaurants, but Estela had only let him cut a window between their kitchens. It was enough of an opening that he could see her cooking whenever he wanted to, but not so much that their restaurants would merge as their lives had.

She'd insisted that what he did was art compared to her simple food. But he never doubted that comfort food was what kept a *Paisa* happy. "To protect your art, there must be a wall between us," she'd insisted. But it was the only part of their lives that stayed separate. She had married him and soon they would have their first child.

And the Americans had come. Sometimes to one restaurant, sometimes to the other. They often brought their friends, which had attracted others, both military and from the city center. Their restaurants had thrived.

But there were only two things that ever passed through the small window between their kitchens.

Estela had insisted that he provide a constant supply of his "magnificent" *obleas* for her customers as well as his own.

And the deck of My Little Pony playing cards, depending on which restaurant the Americans came to eat and play wild games of Truco.

IF YOU ENJOYED THIS, YOU MIGHT
ALSO ENJOY:

WILD JUSTICE (EXCERPT)

The low hill, shadowed by banana and mango trees in the twilight of the late afternoon sun above the Venezuelan jungle, overlooked the heavily guarded camp a half mile away. But that wasn't his immediate problem.

Right now, it took everything Duane Jenkins could do to ignore the stinging sweat dripping into his eyes. Any unwarranted motion or sound might attract his target's attention before he was in position.

From two meters away, he whispered harshly.

"Who the hell are you, sister? And how did you get here?"

"Holy crap!"

He couldn't help but smile. What kind of woman said *crap* when unexpectedly facing a sniper rifle at point-blank range?

"Not your sister," she gained points for a quick recovery. "Now get that rifle out of my face, Jarhead."

Ouch! That was low. He wasn't some damned, swamp-tromping Marine. Not even ex-Marine. He was ex-75th Rangers of the US Army, now two years in Delta Force. And as an operator for The Unit—as Delta called themselves—

that made him far superior to any other soldier no matter what the dudes in SEAL Team 6 thought about it. That also didn't explain who he'd just found here in *the* perfect sniper position overlooking General Raul Estevan Aguado's encampment.

It had taken him over fifteen hours to scout out this one perfect gap between the too-damn-tall trees that made up this sweaty place and, with just twenty meters to go, he'd spotted her heavily camouflaged form lying among the leaves. It had taken him another half hour to cover that distance without drawing her attention.

Where was a cold can of Coke when a guy needed one? This place was worse than Atlanta in the summer. The red earth had been driven so deep into his pores from crawling over the ground that he wondered if his skin color was permanently changed to rust red.

Why did evil bastards like Aguado have to come from such places?

More immediate problem, dude. Stay focused.

The woman's American English was accentless, sounding flat to his Southern ear. Probably from the Pacific Northwest or some other strange part of the country. But there was a thin overlay that matched her Latinate features—full-lipped with dark eyebrows and darker eyes, which was about all he could tell through her camo paint. The slight Spanish lilt shifted her to intriguingly exotic.

But she wasn't supposed to be here. No one was.

"Keeping you in my sights until I get some answers, ma'am," Duane kept his HK MSG90 A2 rifle aimed right at the bridge of her nose—a straight-through spine cutter if he had to take her down. It would be serious overkill, as the weapon was rated to lethal past eight hundred meters and they were whispering at each other from less than two meters apart. With the silencer, his weapon would be even quieter than their whispers, but he hadn't spent the last sixteen hours crawling into position to have her death cry give him away. If she so much as squawked as she went down, every goddamn bird in the jungle would light off, giving away his presence.

She sighed and nodded toward her own rifle that rested on the ground in front of her.

He shifted his focus—though not his aim—then let out a very low whistle of appreciation. A G28. Even his team hadn't gotten their hands on the latest entry into the US Army's sniper arsenal yet. Not quite the same accuracy as his own weapon but six inches shorter, several pounds lighter, and far more flexible to configure. A whole generational leap forward. Richie, his team's tech, would be geeking out right about now. The fact that he wasn't here to see it almost made Duane smile.

"A Heckler & Koch G28. What's your point, sister?" He drawled it out for Richie's sake, who'd be listening in on Duane's radio. Then the implications sank in. If his Delta Force team couldn't get these yet, then who could? Whatever else this woman was, she would be tied to one of the three US Special Mission Units: Delta, SEAL Team 6, or the combat controllers of the Air Force's 24th STS.

Or The Activity.

That fit.

The Intelligence Support Activity served the other three Special Mission Units. If she was with The Activity...that was seriously hot. It meant she was both one of the top intel specialists anywhere *and* a lethal fighter. And that meant that *she'd* been the one to put out the call that had brought him here and was sticking to see the job through. That at least answered why she was in his spot. It also said a lot that she hadn't taken any of several easier-to-reach locations that were almost as good.

"It is about time you caught a clue. Welcome to the conversation." She picked up her rifle as if his wasn't still aimed at her. Very chill. "You are being a little dense there, soldier." At least she got the *branch* of the military right this time.

"Hey, they don't call me 'The Rock' for nothing, darlin'," Duane lowered his barrel until it was pointed into the dirt. "They actually call me that becau—"

The moment his weapon was down, he suddenly was staring down the dark hole of the G28's silencer.

"Uh…"

"The Rock certainly isn't because you are a towering black movie star. It must be for your thick head."

Duane swallowed carefully, unable to shift his focus away from the barrel of her weapon to see if the safety was on or not.

"He spells his name differently. He's Dwayne 'The Rock' with a w and a y. I'm more normal, D-u-a-n-e T-h-e R-o-c-k." He made it sing-song just like the theme song from *The All-New Mickey Mouse Club* that he'd been hooked on as a little kid.

"M-o-u-s-e," she gave the appropriate response.

He couldn't help laughing, quietly, despite their positions —him still staring down the barrel of her weapon—because discovering Mickey Mouse in common in the heart of the Venezuelan jungle was just too funny.

"Normal is not what I need here," the woman sighed and there was the distinct click of her reengaging the safety on her rifle.

"Only thing normal about me is my name, ma'am." Always good to "ma'am" a woman with a sniper rifle pointed at your face.

"Prove it," she turned her weapon once more toward the camp half a kilometer away through the trees. Her motions were appropriately slow to not draw attention. However, it was too even a motion. A sniper learned to never break the pulses of nature's rhythm. She might be some hotshot intel agent—because The Activity absolutely rocked almost everything they did—but she still wasn't Delta, who rocked it all.

Duane breathed out slowly and spent the next couple minutes easing the last two meters toward her. Having the camp in view meant that one of their spotters could see them as well, if the bad guys were damned lucky. He and the woman both wore ghillie suits—that's why he'd gotten so close before he spotted her. The suits were made of open-weave cloth liberally decorated with leaves and twigs so that the two of them looked like little more than a patch of the jungle floor. He'd dragged his on backcountry jungle roads for twenty miles to make sure he smelled like the jungle as well. Having a jaguar trounce his ass wouldn't exactly brighten up his day.

Even their rifles were well camouflaged except for either end of the spotting scopes and the very tips of the barrels. If he hadn't recently been lusting over the new specs, he wouldn't have recognized her HK G28 at all in its disguise.

Getting into position as a sniper took a patience that only the most highly trained could achieve. A female sniper? That was a rare find indeed. The two women on his Delta team were damned fine shooters, but he and Chad were the snipers of the crew. A female sniper from The Activity? This just kept getting better and better. He'd pay a fair wage to know what she really looked like beneath the ghillie and all that face paint.

"Maybe you and I should go to the party as a couple." At long last he lay beside her, close enough that he would have felt her body heat if not for the smothering sauna of his ghillie suit.

"What party? And we're never going to be a couple."

"Halloween. It's only a couple weeks off. We could sneak in and nobody would see us in our ghillies. People would wonder why the punch bowls were mysteriously draining."

"And why the apples were bobbing on their own," she sounded disgusted. "What I want is—"

"Let's see what y'all are up to down there," he cut her off, just for the fun of it, and focused his rifle scope on the camp below. He was a little disappointed when there was no immediate comeback, though there was a low muttering in Spanish that he couldn't quite catch but it cheered his soul.

The general's camp was a simple affair in several ways. The enclosure was a few hundred meters across. An old-school fence of wooden stakes driven into the ground, each a small tree trunk three meters high with sharpened points upward. Not that the points mattered, because razor wire was looped along the top. Guard shacks every hundred meters—four total. The towers straddled the fence. Not a good idea. The structure should have been entirely behind the wall to protect it from attack. Unless...

"You got a name, darling?" Lying beside her, Duane could tell that she was shorter than he was. Her hands were fine, but her body was hidden by the ghillie so he couldn't read anything more about her looks.

"Yes, I have a name."

"That's nice. Always good to have yourself one of those," Duane could play that game just as well as the next person. He turned his attention to the camp. "Our friendly general isn't worried about attack from the outside or he'd have built his towers differently. He's worried about keeping people inside."

***

SOFIA FORTEZA HAD ALREADY KNOWN that from her research,

but she wondered how Duane—spelled the "normal" way—did.

She'd spent months tracking General Aguado. Cripes, she'd spent months finding him in the first place. He was a slippery *bastardo* who did most of his work through intermediaries and only rarely surfaced himself. Tracing him to this corner of the Guatopo National Park—so close to Caracas, the capital of Venezuela, that she'd dismissed it at first—had taken a month more.

Duane had taken one look at the place and seen…what?

He'd have built his towers differently.

She leaned back to her own scope and inspected them again. It took a moment to bring the towers into focus because her nerves were still zinging as if she'd been electrocuted. Somehow, in all her training, she'd never looked down the barrel of a rifle or even a handgun at point blank range— perhaps the scariest thing she'd ever seen.

Scariest other than Duane's cold blue eyes. He was the most dangerous-looking man she'd ever met, which is why his jokes and his smooth Southern accent were throwing her so badly. He sounded half badass, macho-bastard Unit operator and half southern gentleman. It was the strangest combination she'd ever heard. One moment he was wooing her with warm tones, obviously without a clue of how to woo a woman, and the next he was being pure Army grunt with a vocabulary to match. She simply couldn't figure him out.

Finally she shrugged her emotions aside enough to focus her scope properly. *Stay in the jungle, not in your head.* She rebuilt it in layers. The strange silence of the wind—not a single breath of air reached the jungle floor, instead it stagnated, adding to the oppressiveness of the heat. Macaw calls alternated between chatter and screech. Monkeys screamed and shouted in the upper branches. Buzzing flies had learned to leave her alone and the silent ants were no longer creeping her out. All that was left after she canceled each of those out was the man breathing beside her and the compound of that bastard Aguado that she'd been staring at for the last twenty-four hours.

The guard towers were supported by four long, tree-trunk legs, two inside the fence and two outside. Outside! Where they were vulnerable to attack. General Aguado hadn't built a fort in the depths of a national park—he'd built a prison.

All of her research had only uncovered his location, not his purpose here. Because she hadn't cared. Cutting the head off the snake one target at a time worked for her.

She looked again at the camp. Wooden shacks for the most part—workers' cabins. What else had she missed?

"Locks on the doors," Duane answered the question she hadn't asked in a whisper that was surprisingly soft for such a deep voice. He ignored a fer-de-lance pit viper as it slid up and over the ghillie covering his rifle barrel, slowing to inspect them with a flick of its tongue before continuing on its way in search of mice. If he could ignore the snake, so could she. Mostly. A little. She watched long after it had slithered out of sight.

Sofia looked at the shacks' doors again. Locks on the *outside*. She'd been watching the camp for twenty-four hours and had missed that. The dozens of armed guards weren't being lazy on patrol as she'd thought. They didn't care about the outside world—they were worried about the inside one. And because they were the only armed personnel in the camp, and everyone knew it, they could afford to be nonchalant.

Back to the towers. The guards were leaning on the inside rails looking down, not the outside ones looking out. All of her work to slip into this position was probably meaningless.

If Duane was right, she could walk right up and knock on the front gate before anyone would pay her the least attention. A band of red howler monkeys working their way noisily through the jungle canopy above the camp didn't even attract a glance from the guards.

Still, Aguado was here. She'd seen him arrive with his entourage. And he was never going to leave. Not alive.

"Not a nice place," Duane observed quietly.

"Not a nice man."

"Sure I am. You just don't know me yet, sugar."

Sofia brought her knee up sharply. Lying side by side, she was able to bullseye the Charlie-horse nerve cluster on his outer thigh. Her nana hadn't raised her to be a target.

"Shit!" He didn't sound so almighty pleased with himself any longer, though he did manage to keep it to a whisper as he continued swearing.

Why did guys always think they were so charming? With her looks, she should be used to it by now. Except her looks were hidden by the ghillie suit. What had kicked Duane-spelled-the-normal-way into such a guy mode? Just that she was female? When did Delta start recruiting cavemen as their standard? Actually, that one she knew the answer to—since Day One if past experience meant anything.

She hadn't ever deployed with Delta before, but she'd met enough of them to know the type. They were the rebel super-warriors of the US military. Everyone thought that their team was the baddest, but Delta Force, more commonly called "The Unit," completely owned that title. Somehow they drew the people that didn't fit anywhere else in the military. But where they'd been troublemakers in their old units, 1st Special Forces Operational Detachment-Delta collected them and honed their skills. They were like a barely controlled reaction just bubbling along, waiting for an excuse to explode.

"So, what's the general's story?" Duane, once he was done nursing his thigh, went for a subject change proving he wasn't stupid.

"Deep in the drug trade. Known to have called for at least three high profile murders, including a Supreme Tribunal of Justice judge (that's their version of the Supreme Court) even if he didn't pull the trigger himself."

"Oh, so *he's* the one that's not nice," as if Duane only now was figuring that out.

She was not going to be charmed by him. His every tone said that just because she was female, he'd switched into some weird-ass flirt mode. She'd had enough of that coming up through the ranks to last a lifetime.

"This isn't slave labor, so you'd better add human trafficking to your list." With the speed of a light switch, all the charm was gone from Duane's voice.

As if to prove his point, at that moment a couple of guards exited a small building, readjusting their pants and laughing. They kicked the door shut behind them and snapped the lock closed. No question what they'd just been doing to some poor women—one of the perks of their job.

Numerous guards. Locks on the outside of the cabin doors. No large central building that might be an illicit drug lab or slave labor textile sweatshop. This was a holding pen, hidden deep in the jungle of a national park. The few people who were circulating around, aside from the guards, were almost all women. Women who were keeping their heads down and trudging about their tasks. The sickness that twisted in her stomach had nothing to do with lying still for the last twenty-four hours.

Sofia wasn't even aware of raising her rifle until Duane reached over and casually pushed it back down.

"Not yet." It was all he said, but she could hear the anger beneath the soft words.

Well that wasn't shit compared to what *she* was feeling at the moment. This place needed to be erased from the map. Scorched to the ground, removed permanently from existence!

"Why are you here? I sent for a goddamn team, not some Southern Rock."

He flashed a smile at her, "If you've got me, you don't need a team." All of his macho bravado was back. As if she'd misheard his momentary anger. He sounded too much like her useless brother and the rest of her useless family. She couldn't be rid of him fast enough.

As the last of the sunlight faded from the sky and the bird calls tapered toward silence, Sofia wondered who she was going to want to shoot more by sunrise: General Raul Estevan Aguado or Duane The Rock?

Available at fine retailers everywhere

ABOUT THE AUTHOR

M.L. Buchman started the first of, what is now over 50 novels and even more short stories, while flying from South Korea to ride his bicycle across the Australian Outback. Part of a solo around the world trip that ultimately launched his writing career.

Three times, his titles have been named "Top 10 Romance of the Year" by the American Library Association's *Booklist*. NPR and Barnes & Noble have named other titles "Top 5 Romance of the Year." In 2016 he was a finalist for Romance Writers of America prestigious RITA award. He also writes: contemporary romance, thrillers, and fantasy.

Past lives include: years as a project manager, rebuilding and single-handing a fifty-foot sailboat, both flying and jumping out of airplanes, and he has designed and built two houses. He is now making his living as a full-time writer on the Oregon Coast with his beloved wife and is constantly amazed at what you can do with a degree in Geophysics. You may keep up with his writing and receive a free novel by subscribing to his newsletter at: www.mlbuchman.com

Join the conversation:
www.mlbuchman.com

Other works by M. L. Buchman: